McDUFF
MOVES IN

ROSEMARY WELLS • SUSAN JEFFERS

HYPERION BOOKS FOR CHILDREN
NEW YORK

In the back of a dogcatcher's truck
sat a little white dog nobody wanted.

Thump! went the truck over a bump in the road.
The little dog popped out into the night.

He tumbled onto the soft earth of a tulip bed.
He did not know where he was.

He needed something to eat.
He needed a warm place to sleep.
So he went looking.

"*Woof!*" said the little white dog at the front door
of number six Pine Road. But the answer from
the other side was, "*GROWL!*"

"Woof!" he said on the front steps of number twelve
Oak Lane. But someone said, *"Hiss!"* from the woodpile.

Strange voices hooted and whistled at him
from the trees.

Many pairs of eyes winked and blinked at him from
the darkness of people's gardens.

Rain poured down.
It swirled and swept around him.

Suddenly the wind came up.
It blew the clouds and rain away.

And the moon smiled full on the world. Through an open window in the kitchen of number seven Elm Road wafted the smell of vanilla rice pudding and sausages.

"Woof! Woof! Woof!" said the little white dog.

Nobody growled at him. Nobody hissed at him.
Somebody opened the door and asked him to come in.
It was Lucy. "This is Fred," said Lucy.

No one had ever asked him to come in.
Everyone had always told him to go away.

"What does his collar say?" asked Fred.
"Animal number forty-seven . . . city dog pound," said Lucy.
"He needs help," said Fred.

Lucy spooned out a dish of vanilla rice pudding.
She sliced sausages on top of it. "He's hungry," she said.

After a coconut herbal bath he looked like a snow cloud.
"We certainly can't keep him," Fred said.
"We're much too busy."

"I guess we'll have to take him to the dog pound,"
said Lucy. So they brought him into the car.

Fred drove up and down and around.
"You are going in circles, Fred," said Lucy.

"I don't want to find the dog pound," said Fred.
"I don't want you to find it," said Lucy.

Fred and Lucy brought their new friend home.
"All he needs is a name," said Fred.
They celebrated with hot chocolate.

Lucy opened a tin of McDuff's Melt in Your Mouth
Shortbread Biscuits. "That's it!" said Fred.
"Woof Woof!" said McDuff.

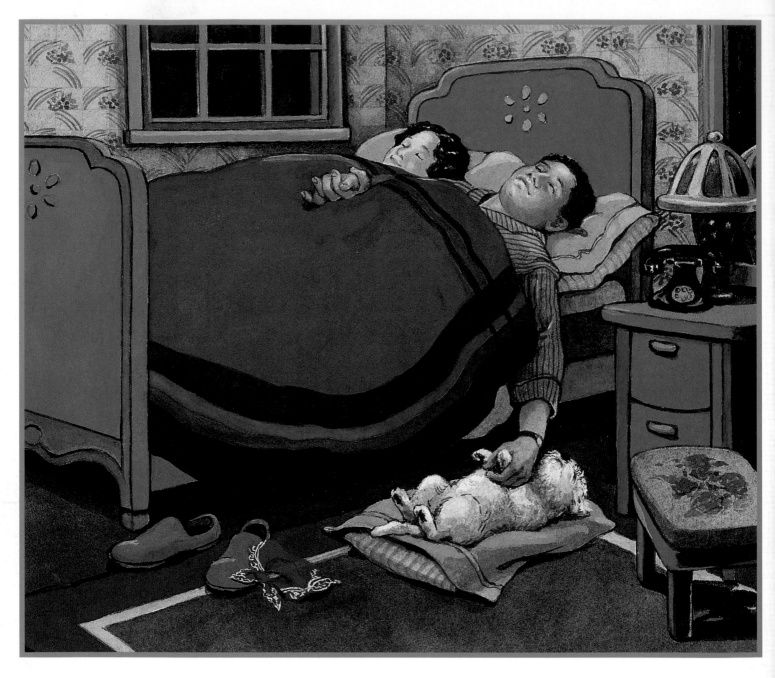

The night was nearly gone.
The rain clattered and spattered over everything.
Lucy and Fred and McDuff fell sound asleep.
"How happy we are!" they said in their dreams.

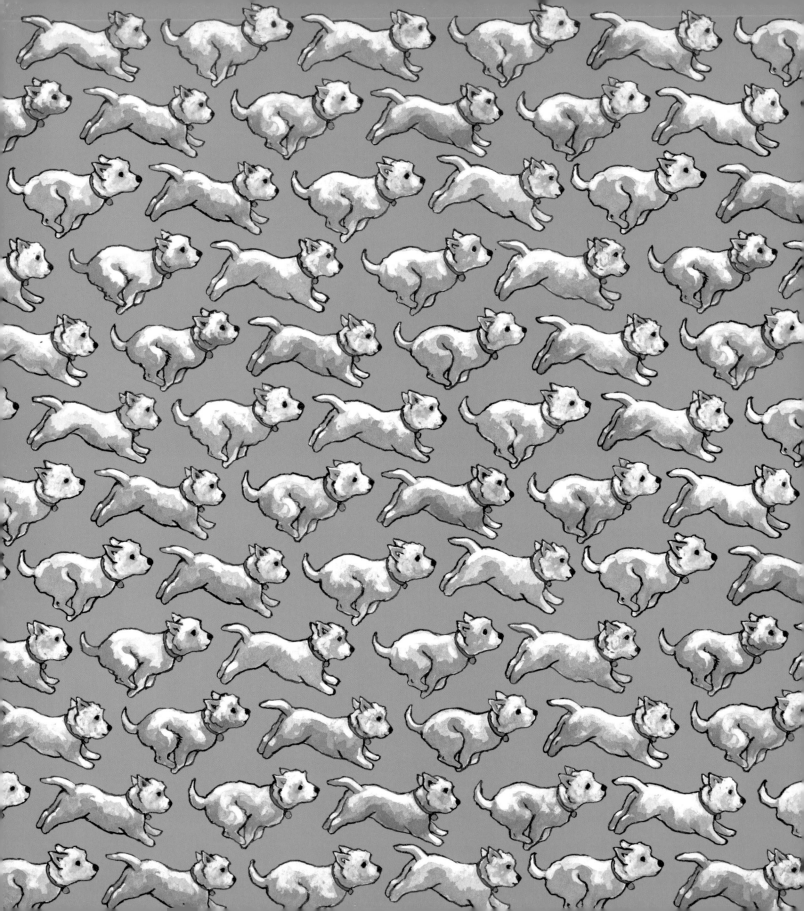